Pixie's Holidays

Emmanuelle Payot Karpathakis

summertimepublishing

Published in Great Britain 2013 by Summertime Publishing
© Copyright Emmanuelle Payot Karpathakis

ISBN 978-1-909193-25-3

Creative Director Graham Booth of www.creationbooth.com

To my beloved four children and my husband.

Thanks to Ricardo for his beautiful illustrations as well as
Jo and Graham!

Thank you Mom, Dad and all my expat friends who helped me.

One morning a beautiful sun is warming our pretty little Pixie. Leaving her house she goes to her friend Dido's house. It is still very early, but Pixie knows that her friend is awake. He is waiting for her because they have decided to go for a walk near the river.

"Hi Dido, I'm ready, let's go! Come on, hurry up!"

"Well, you're very excited! Calm down, I'm coming! Why are you such in hurry?"

"I've got to tell you about Daddy's big project. You'll be very surprised! Let's go! Shall we gallop?"

The two friends run as fast as their tiny hooves can carry them, disturbing the butterflies and crushing the flowers under their feet.

By the time they arrive at the river, Pixie is completely out of breath. Her friend gallops so fast! Several times she lost sight of him!

"So, what's this great news, Pixie?"

"Yesterday evening, I heard Mommy and Daddy talking about our holidays. We're going to visit my friend Lila. Isn't it wonderful! I'm going to see my best friend again!"

"But I thought that you had forgotten her."

"Yes, well… no… er… I don't remember her face, her wings or her feathers very well. But, anyway, I will be so happy to see her again. She must have missed me."

Dido grumbles a bit. He feels a little pinch of jealousy growing in his heart. Pixie is going to leave him. Who will he race with now?

"When are you leaving?"

"Tomorrow. It's supposed to be a surprise, but I heard everything. I must go. Mommy and Daddy are waiting for me. Bye!"

Dido doesn't even have time to say goodbye to Pixie: she has already left. He sighs.

At home, her parents are very busy. Three suitcases are ready in the hallway.

"Mommy, Daddy, what are you doing? Are we going on a trip?"

"Yes my dear, tomorrow morning. And guess where?"

"To see my friend Lila?"

"Yes, sweetie. We'll spend some time close to our old pasture. And we'll see your grandma too."

"Yippee! That's great! Thanks Mommy. Thank you Daddy!"

"You need to get your cuddly ready and have a good night's sleep. We will have a long journey tomorrow."

Pixie spends the rest of the day, dreaming. She tries to remember Lila, but the picture in her mind is foggy; it's also hard to remember their games. The garden, the house – she has forgotten almost everything. Only Grandma is still clear in her memory, because they have spoken to each other regularly on the phone. This evening Pixie is very excited and finds it hard to sleep.

Next morning, Pixie's parents put the luggage and their daughter in the cart pulled by Patouf, a great big horse. Pixie says goodbye happily to Dido, who is trying not to cry. He has never been apart from her for a year, but his friend seems so eager to get away from here.

It's a long journey and Pixie falls asleep.

She wakes up abruptly when the cart stops. Patouf neighs happily. His job is done.

Pixie looks around her curiously. Where is her friend Lila? Is this really where she used to live? Everything seems strange, different; nothing is anything like her few memories.

"Mommy, where are we?"

"In front of our old pasture, darling."

"Are we going to sleep here?"

"No, when we left, we gave our garden to another family, and they live here now."

Pixie is not really sad – she just does not feel at home here. Her parents are happy and delighted to meet their friends again. They move away chatting happily with them and Pixie finds herself alone at the edge of the field.

Suddenly she hears laughter from behind a bush. She goes closer and sees a little lamb jumping all over the place. A goose is waddling after him.

"Theo! Wait for me!" screams the goose. "You're going too fast! It's not fair!"

"Ha-ha! Can't catch me, Lila! Use your wings!"

Lila! Pixie cannot believe it! She has discovered her friend! But she stays hidden, so she can watch the two who are playing together.

They are playing leapfrog and Theo suddenly finds himself in front of Pixie. He's quite surprised.

"Hi, my name's Theo," he says. "Who are you?"

"Pixie."

"Lila, come and see! There's a little donkey here."

Curiously, Lila comes closer and asks, "What's your name?"

"Pixie."

"Pixie. What a cute name! So, Theo, shall we get on with our game?"

Pixie is very disappointed. She may not remember her friend's appearance very well, but at least she knows her name!

Head drooping, she comes back to her parents. The grown-ups are laughing a lot; they are surrounded by their friends and family.

"Pixie, sweetheart, come and say hello. Everyone would like to see you."

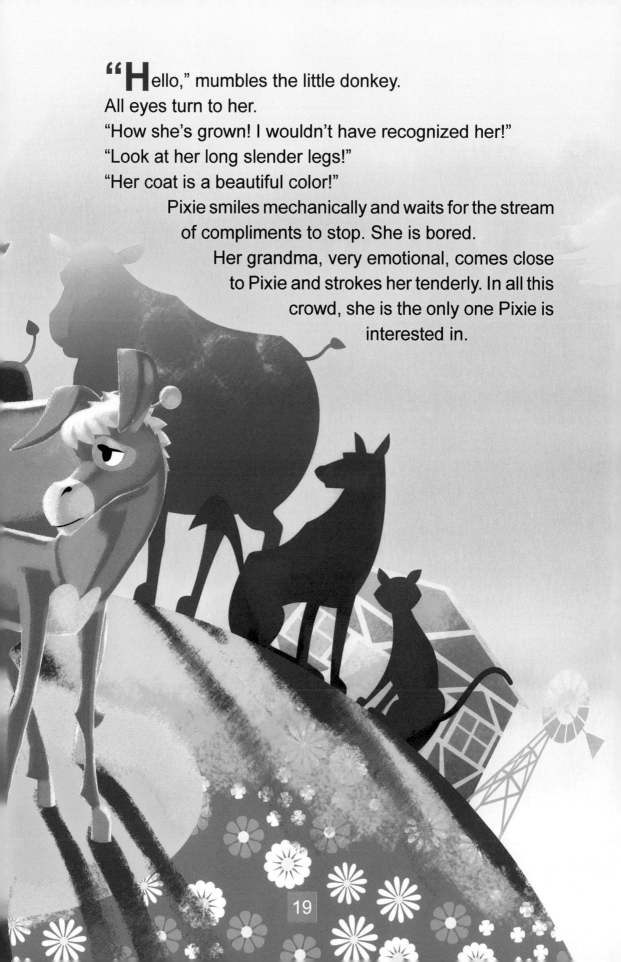

"**H**ello," mumbles the little donkey.

All eyes turn to her.

"How she's grown! I wouldn't have recognized her!"

"Look at her long slender legs!"

"Her coat is a beautiful color!"

Pixie smiles mechanically and waits for the stream of compliments to stop. She is bored.

Her grandma, very emotional, comes close to Pixie and strokes her tenderly. In all this crowd, she is the only one Pixie is interested in.

19

At night, Pixie is still grumpy. Her daddy is worried. "What's wrong Pixie?" he asks.

"Do we have to stay here long?"

"Yes, why? Don't you like it here? When you were young, you loved this countryside."

"I don't remember anything and I don't have any friends anymore," complained Pixie."

"Haven't you seen Lila?"

"Lila doesn't even recognize my name and she has a new friend!"

Pixie's daddy suddenly understands why his daughter is so sad.

"Lila was very young when you left. You would have forgotten her, too, but we talked about her often and you wanted to see her again, didn't you?"

"Mmm, yes. But didn't she care about me? She doesn't even know my name!"

"Maybe nobody talked about you during the year, so her memories completely vanished. Tomorrow we'll go to see her, OK?"

"If you like," sighs Pixie.

The next morning, Daddy and Pixie go out into the big pasture. Lila and Theo are already playing leapfrog.

Daddy calls to Lila, "Lila, can you come here for a minute, please?"

"Yes, Sir. Coming!"

"Do you know Pixie?" asks Daddy.

"Yes, I met her yesterday," replies Lila.

"But you've known her for a long time! Before we moved away, she was your friend."

"What?"

"Yes, a year ago she was even your best friend."

Lila is very surprised; nobody had talked to her about Pixie. Her best friend is Theo.

"Were you really my friend before?" she asks Pixie.

"Yes, and I would like to play with you again," Pixie tells her.

"But you are too big for me and Theo is softer!" says Lila.

Theo interrupts. "Lila, don't be angry! Of course Pixie can play with us. Come on, let's have a race!"

The three runners race away. Pixie naturally gets in front of the lamb and the goose, who is angry and waddles furiously. She does not like to lose! Cunningly she proposes another game: hide and seek.

Then it's the donkey who has a big problem because the only bush in the pasture is small and Theo is already hiding there, so Pixie is often the one who has to count.

Theo feels sorry for her but Lila is very glad!

"How about we stop playing?" he suggests. "Let's go and rest for a while and have something to eat."

"After all that, Theo is the nicest," thinks Pixie.

In the late afternoon, Mommy comes back from her visits to her friends feeling very happy.

"How are you, honey?"

"Huh! Lila is not very nice to me. I like Theo better," says Pixie.

"Maybe Lila is scared that you'll take her friend away," suggests Mommy.

"Lila was supposed to be my true friend. Now I hate her!" sulks Pixie, and she thinks of Dido, whom she loves so much. Suddenly she misses him a lot!

Grandma comes to talk to Pixie.

"In life, we change houses, we leave our family, we part from our friends," she explains. "But then meeting new people makes us very happy too. Haven't you spoken to me about Dido? If Lila came come to your house maybe Dido would be jealous, or you would ignore Lila to play with him. New friendships are always coming along and Theo seems to like you."

Pixie goes to bed thinking about Grandma's words. It was hard to meet a different, almost unknown Lila. The two old friends have nothing in common anymore. On the other hand, Theo is really attentive to Pixie.

The days go by quickly. Pixie plays all the time with Theo and Lila who is always as cranky as she was at first, and it's Theo who is the leader of the game.

Today, he suggests a new game: jumping obstacles. Everyone ought to have a chance of winning: Pixie can stride over, Lila can shake her wings and Theo can bounce on his fine legs. The one who doesn't manage to get across the obstacle loses.

The game begins. At first, Theo chooses a few low branches, which are easy to get over, but then it gets more difficult: the obstacles get higher and more twisted. Lila has trouble and runs out of steam.

"Serves her right!" thinks Pixie, "Meanness is always punished!"

Suddenly the goose wants to land, stumbles and falls into a woodpile, which collapses. Theo stops immediately. Pixie slows down and smiles quietly to herself.

Lila does not get up. Worried, the two friends come close and discover her under a big branch. She is stuck and she's crying.

"My wing hurts very badly! I can't move it!"

Theo and Pixie don't know what to do. The lamb is sad because he is too small to help his friend.

The donkey hesitates. "I think I can help you," she says. "I am big enough. I'm going to come close to you and move some branches away, then I'll try to lift you gently."

She gets to work and removes some of the pieces of wood round Lila. Then, she puts her head down between the goose's webbed feet and tells her to try and climb up her forehead. Lila rises, struggles up and settles, moaning, between the two eyes of Pixie. It is such a funny sight that Theo can't help bursting out laughing.

"Stop it, Theo! Instead of standing there laughing, come and help me! You need to guide me. I can hardly see a thing!"

Very slowly, Pixie, Lila on top of her head, and Theo head to the barn. It's a very funny parade, which crosses the meadow.

Pixie slowly lowers her head and lays Lila down on a haystack. Her wing is very sore, but at last she can rest and stay still.

"Thank you for your help Pixie! If it hadn't been for you, I would still be stuck there."

Pixie is a bit ashamed of what she'd been thinking. "Think nothing of it! Friends must help each other if they have an accident," she says.

"Then, thank you for being my friend," says Lila and smiles at Pixie for the first time since her arrival.

The next few weeks go by very quickly and the vacation is almost finished.

Lila has been well taken care of. She has a cast on her wing but it does not prevent her from waddling around and running with the others. Pixie and Theo spend a lot of time with her. Sometimes they remember Lila's "rescue" and laugh a lot! A new friendship has been born and the next vacation promises to be full of fun!

When the time comes to leave, Pixie cries loudly: now there are two friends she has to leave! However, she can't wait to see Dido and tell him all about her adventures.

Her grandmother whispers to her, "These holidays have helped you to build a new friendly relationship with Lila and Theo. At home you'll meet Dido again, your everyday best friend. Take care of these friendships because they will be very precious in your life."

THE END

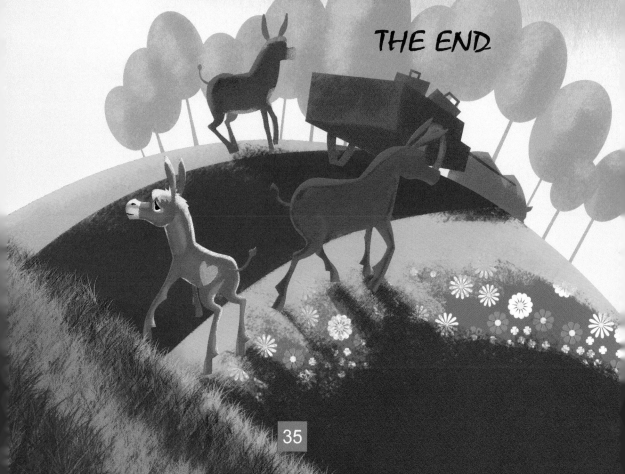

Put some color on Pixie and her friends :

Find the differences (they are ten) :

Emmanuelle Payot Karpathakis has experienced both expatriation and repatriation. To date she has lived with her family in five countries. She is now in Greece with her husband and four children. While in Geneva she worked for seven years as a senior relocation adviser and is now an independent consultant and relocation coach. Emmanuelle also writes stories for young expatriates! *Pixie's Holidays* is the sequel to *Pixie's New Home*. Her family is trilingual and so it is no surprise that the Pixie series of books are translated into six languages – English, French, German, Spanish, Portuguese and Russian.

Emmanuelle Payot Karpathakis
Writer, Relocation coach

Expatskids Payot
65 ch. Du Cannelet
1285 Avusy- Geneva
T: 0030 22410 021 28
M: 0030 695 940 20 91
info@expatskids.com | www.expatskids.com

Next Book:

Pixie's
Dad gets a New Job

CPSIA information can be obtained
at www.ICGtesting.com
Printed in the USA
LVIC040501040313

322495LV00001B